ANOTHER ROUND
IN ANOTHER DIVE

poems, essays, and short stories

by Lanser Howard and Steve Boint

Scurfpea
Publishing L.L.C.

First edition 2025.
ISBN: 979-8-9928848-0-7

Cover photograph by Mike Kelley.
Cover page block print by Steve Boint. *Full Circle*. 8"×10".
Back cover photographs by Lanser Howard
                except for photograph 5 which is by Karen Dunbar.

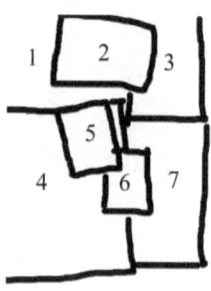

Scurfpea Publishing
P.O. Box 46
Sioux Falls, SD 57101
scurfpeapublishing.com
editor@scurfpeapublishing.com

Contents

The Red Frog

Up in the Sierras
off Interstate 80
the Red Frog
sits
waits
for the action
to come.

A mix
of mountain men
bikers
artists
good, blue collar
folk
that carry only
cash.

Day to day
livin'
is really something.

Most don't understand.

You ride the wind
because
that is all
you have
to carry you
to the next day.

Good company
strong drinks
no BS
only
wind riders.

A docked ship sits
out front
a reminder of where
you were going
before
you got grounded
by reality.

Catch lightning
when the weather
hits
the deck out back
overlooking
wide open possibility.

Sierra Nevada
dreamin'
within reach
now
gone south
caught
by the Red Frog.

Security is a
wonderful
cozy place
ambition
held captive
only
by fear.

– Lanser Howard

Louisa's Place

Knives out!
Two against one on the back deck.
You,
me,
about 15 others dive inside to "safety."
The bartender,
whose key chain outweighs her,
grabs a broom,
runs the opposite way.

Us heroes crowd a window to watch
three figures flee down the rutted alley
and hear that bartender,
swirling her broom overhead,
Come back if you want more!

I love this place.

– Steve Boint

Wagon Wheel Bar

The neon lady reclined three stories above
asphalt with gravel-filled potholes,
on an Old-West wagon wheel,
shirt buttons unused.

Never once, when biking past,
did I see female patrons enter or leave.
Grizzled guys in worn clothes regularly climbed
from or into beat up Fords or Chevrolets.

I moved away before aging enough to venture inside.
Just as well. I can almost believe
it was bad timing on my part.
The mystery and lust-filled dream remains.

– Steve Boint

Bill's Place

Honest place
honest men
honest pours
Bill's Place
a prohibition era
joint
where moonshine
was once brewed in the basement
below
a place
of no bullshit
no time
for
pretension here.

Belly up to the bar
hang your hat
on elk horns
and get to drinkin'.

Busy day drinkin'
bars
know the struggle
of shift work.

You can FEEL
people thinking
here
drinks to forget
about the day
wasted
workin' for the man

drinks
to make it easier
to go home.

Freedom rains
a wagon wheel and AK-47
sit in the corner
as a reminder
of the struggle and
journey
to get here.

Original owners
bought the bar
with World War I
enlistment bonus money.

Bill's Place
is the place
you
can always go
when
there is no place
to go
when you
can't
go home.

– Lanser Howard

Clammy booths and a string of lights
don't make a dive bar,
but what does?

Guy in the corner
behind the dead ficus twitches
while playing Willie on a ukulele.

All sorts of insects here.
Small packages passed
through handshakes or hugs.

I watch the game.
Two lumps of loose clothing
sit at the bar and watch a different one.

Angry voices from dark tables, and
I pay my tab, exit
past old panhandlers surrounding the door.

That door is featureless plate steel,
no sign to advertise the bar is here.
No one will miss it when it isn't.

– Steve Boint

Hell Creek Bar

People come here
for lack of a there.
Old stone walls
halt ever-wandering dust,
except near windows
where old panes rattle.
Cool inside
compared to outside.
Greasy food,
but it's tough to ruin canned beer.
Cardboard sign at the counter
promises a new fridge is on order:

COMING IN SEPTEMBER – COLD BEER!

– Steve Boint

On Spinners and Spinees

On its back, a dead cockroach spins
counterclockwise on the counter.
As spinner of the spinee, he watches.
No one else pays close enough attention
to anyone or anything else
to realize
that
spinning between beers
is a marvel
or at least a mystery.
How did it croak?
It wasn't squished.
Wouldn't be poisoned . . . here.
Do roaches die of old age?
Doin' alright, buddy?
as the bartender's stained towel
pulls that insect away.

– Steve Boint

After Smo's Bar Died

Pockmarked reflections
puddle on the concrete patio.
Last summer's plants slump
brittle inside pots stacked
beside this beaded glass door.
Haven't seen you since
they flattened the old place.
Thought rain might bring you
to some beer-flavored window.
Not here – obviously. It's clean,
well-manicured with no culture.
Not like us or the old place;
nothing is.

– Steve Boint

The Crows Nest

Trust me
folks don't sip
around here.

No tinkling of
wine glasses or
toasting of cocktails . . .

all you hear
is the sliding of barstools
and that all-too-
familiar
clank
down
of shot glass
on hardwood.

And this place has
locals only
rough and ready
no tourists
only working men
worn and weathered
from working the Atlantic.

Men that have been
riding giants
and pulling crab lines
for months.

I will tell you
one secret
in this place
the hands
tell you
all you
need to know
about a man
and sometimes
the lines on the face
give you
vivid backstory.

Pour it straight here.

For God's sake
do NOT
order a cocktail
nobody has time for such
tomfoolery.

– Lanser Howard

AI
old Acapulco Inn

You can put
lipstick on a pig
AI
is proof.

Times change
she is all
dressed up now.

Going back . . .
it was a dimly lit
dive
always packed
Christmas lights
up
year-round
the madness
the sloppiness
every Friday and Saturday
night
this Long Beach
watering hole
was always the spot
to get the party
crackin'

and often the
last stop
spot
with the most famous
last call drink:

THE Guttershot.

A glorious concoction
of spillover pours
leftover
from the gutter of the bar.

Easy to serve up
dip the shot glass
in the gutter rail
and serve.

You get your
beer
plus
EVERY beer back
all
in one shot.

– Lanser Howard

Afternoon Dive

Lazily spinning ceiling fans
sway an off-axis dance.
Slowly swings the flag outside
as a waltz limps from counter speakers.
Bourbon floods my soul mellow.

– Steve Boint

In July

Thirty-one people,
'bout half full,
at the Triangle Bar on Saturday,
darktime . . .
and that's counting the wooden cigar girl
and two people driving past on a Harley.
The Burlington Northern and Santa Fe rolls by
twenty feet away. Shakes the floor.
Still, the band plays frantically
as the crowd claps,
shouts,
gyrates.
Maybe they're more than half full.

– Steve Boint

Hell's Angel High

It all started out doing Crown shots. Shot only drinking generally ends bad. This almost did. One hard, fast rule I've learned when hanging with outlaws or gangsters is things can pop off quickly and you can find yourself caught in their jackpot quicker. Beware and pay attention to eyes on you and bounce BEFORE things get sticky.

"I've ridden all over Alaska, watched the Northern Lights doing 120 on the back of a Harley in the middle of nowhere."

"Yeah, I've heard Alaska is pretty amazing. Haven't had a chance to get up there yet."

"I live in Homer, about four hours outside of Anchorage. If you come up, I'll show you around."

"Well I don't ride."

"Fuck it, you can follow me in your little rental car."

We both laughed.

"Can we go fishin'."

"What do you f-ing think."

Joe looked like a grizzly bear. 6'4" and wide as a semi . . . you could hit him with a board, and he wouldn't flinch. Tatted sleeves and had a laugh that made the walls shake. A Hell's Angel from Alaska. And yes, he looked the part.

"Give us another round!"

Joe stamped his empty shot glass down onto the

bar. I noticed the barkeep was losing his patience and eyes from the back table were squarely upon us. Shots arrived and shots disappeared.

"My lady, would you like to join us," Joe asked.

Michelle, my beautiful photographer friend always gets invited to these soirees. She looked at Joe a bit hesitant and didn't answer.

"Alright," I said. "Let's have a chat about it."

We all got up and filed out of the bar and probably shouldn't have set up shop out front.

"I'll take ya to private land waters. Salmon the f-ing size of Moby Dick," Joe exhales a smokestack worth of smoke. "F-ing beautiful land up there. God's country."
"I've been hearing that for years, gotta get up there," I said. "What about the snow?"

I motioned to his Harley parked on the street.

"How the hell do you travel around on that thing when it's below zero?"
"I live off the back of that thing. One time, comin' back from Texas in January, rollin' over the Sierras, snow storm hit before I could find a motel . . . so had to spend the night in the belly of a dumpster."
"Guess you gotta take what you can get sometimes?"
"Sometimes? I've done it many times on cross country runs in the dead of winter."

Silence as we sat there passing the blunt around.

"I'm moving 365 days a year on the road, so I know all the small towns, remote towns, places civilians can't go to. Know what I mean?"

"Is that how you found this place?"

The Miner's Club in Georgetown, California is in the Sierra Nevada mountains, about 1 ½ hours west of Lake Tahoe. Nobody rolls through here, way off the beaten path on Highway 193.

"I had a job in Reno and just picked a place off the 80."

"Joe, Georgetown ain't so close to the 80."

"Well, I got a lady friend over in Pilot Hill . . . and one in Cool too."

We laughed as Big Joe took another monster hit off the magic cigar.

"You know, Lans, I don't like many people, even my friends think I'm a mean son-of-a-bitch."

"Well Joe, I ain't your friend."

We laughed again as a car door slammed, off in the distance. Joe suddenly got distracted. We kept talking but it was if he was a million miles away. His eyes narrowed and it wasn't from the weed. It was from a seasoned, always paranoid place you need to live in all the time, when you live Joe's life.

It didn't help the surly bartender peeked his head outside, checking on our whereabouts.

Joe was no longer fun to be around. He was staring unblinkingly at the window upstairs across the street. I noticed the blinds split open earlier.

And just like that, Joe walked across the street, fired up his hog and sped off.

Didn't say a word. Left us mid-sentence with a Hell's Angel high.

– Lanser Howard

Barely Familiar

These alleys have changed,
turned to smoking dens
behind high-end restaurants and trendy bars.
But don't trust them –
still they run with vagrant blood,
now from the thousand paper cuts
of investment group accountants.

– Steve Boint

Piety

I volunteered for a group that carried food and coffee out on the streets for Philadelphia's homeless. One evening, we approached a disheveled man sitting on a bus stop bench just outside a bar. He jumped up and ran towards us, shouting, "Thank God you're here."

He stopped, looked at me and asked urgently, "Would you hold my Bible?" So I reached out with one hand to receive a tattered King James translation.

Before any of us could even wish him a good evening, he turned and ran into the bar.

We stood out there. After about five minutes, we discussed going in to get him, but decided he might be in the restroom.

Ten minutes later, he came back out smiling, "Thank you, thank you, thank you. I needed that drink, but didn't want to leave my Bible out here where it would get stolen. And I sure couldn't take the word of God in THERE."

– Steve Boint

Shaky

Philly is a heartless city if you have no money. So, I took winter interim off from attending grad school and got a job outside Newark, clear-cutting trees to make room for a strip mall. Developers are devils . . . but they have money.

I hadn't run a chainsaw since high school so, by morning of the second day, I could barely grip my rusted Chevette's steering wheel. It only got worse as the day progressed. Heading home, I realized I would cross Ben Franklin Bridge AT RUSH HOUR; shifting the standard transmission and steering would require working hands, so . . . I pulled into a tired little bar named Howard's.

I had enough money for the bridge when I headed home and one orange juice I hoped to nurse for an hour. Driving with no hands is not a time for alcohol.

I was the only customer. A sullen, slovenly man with three days' growth of beard lurked behind the counter. He looked at me funny when I ordered the orange juice, but gave it to me. Then he walked over to a jukebox I hadn't noticed, punched a button, music kicked on as he yelled "Beatrice!" then walked away.

I jumped when, a little to my left and behind the bar, a curtain swished open and out danced a veiled lady. Now, I don't know veils from scarves, but it was pretty clear I was to lay down bills and scarves/veils would fall.

No money was forthcoming. Nothing interesting got revealed. Shortly, she flipped her hair, gave a sniff, and stalked back behind the curtain. I couldn't drink the orange juice, my exhausted hands shaking too badly from the chainsaw. Seemed a good time to walk out.

Sat in my car for another 45 minutes. No one else pulled in.

– Steve Boint

Holy Diver

Dig deeper
find that place
where you know
within it
all
nothing shines
brighter
than
your place in
the sun
sitting in
your dive spot
high
as you can
dream
but never
enough
for your ambition.

– Lanser Howard

Question

Outside the door, a planet bakes.
Inside, in here, it's cold enough to freeze flies.
Or maybe those slow bugs found
one of the many beer rings
and slurped,
and slurped,
and slurped.
How much beer is needed
to render a fly unflightworthy?

– Steve Boint

Pass the Bag

Can we go back
to blazing out for the weekend
ridin' the rising sun
on that one way road
to opportunity
orange
desert dry
and a thirst for adventure?

Rollin' in @ 6 am
catchin' luck
last spot
in the casino parking lot.

It's go time.

We brown-bagged it
pass the bottle.

Started in Reno
then graduated to
Vegas
when we
had more dough
livin' fast
hard wreckin'
some in our wake
but g-dammit
we had a good time.

Hittin' 16 @ Binion's
catchin' half the time
it didn't matter
we had youth and good luck
on our sides . . .
booze and friends
what more
could we ask for?

Throw in some music
pass the bag PT
let's do it again brother.

Welcome to sin city.

Always
grasping for something
better
than this 9-5
Monday through Friday
life.

Lest us forget
simpler times
when we
brown bagged it
under those blinking lights.

We
had
it
all.

– Lanser Howard

Time to Go

The city of brotherly love, where goodwill does not extend to providing public restrooms. It was a hot day and I was stomping north between Chestnut and Market, east of City Hall. Solid buildings like cliffs along the sunny side of the street. No windows. No real doors on the block, except for one, and I needed to find a restroom sooner than riding a bus home would allow. That door, a green-painted sheet of steel on hinges, had a bland name, O'Malley's or something like that. Probably a pub, so I walked up to the door and pulled it open.

I stood inside a narthex; the bouncer said, $10. Steep, but urgently worthwhile. I paid the cover, walked through to a loud, dark room as the door shut behind me.

Flashing lights and pounding music. Poles holding naked women. A sea of unwelcoming faces. I was the only pale person there and judged that restroom well beyond reach.

I stepped back through the door. The bouncer held the outer door for me. Back on the street . . . without bus fare.

– Steve Boint

Patience

Do you look for me?
I'm here where wine drinkers aren't.

Let my beard grow
and shaved my head.
This city is dark;
trouble dogs the visible.

Heady months, weren't they?
Pretend control but just hang on.

Sadly, life isn't a bull ride.
Takes months, years maybe,
to dismount and all the time
life keeps bucking . . . .
Land on your feet
or get there fast
then run like hell.

I hide behind this table, now.
Someday I'll shave
and find you;
if you'll let me.
We could reminisce.
I'd like that.

– Steve Boint

Coloma Club

Saturday watched
rain splatter
fluorescent glass
storm
rollin' in
tip the bottle
back
more music
less talk.

Come on over
baby girl
sit on my lap
c'mon
baby girl
pull your hair
back
tilt your seat
back
lick my whiskey
lips
ready for the
night's
trip.

One roller coaster
ride
I promise
you
won't forget.

– Lanser Howard

Hit the Floor, Jack

Some young guy with a bad haircut
mumbles into the mic
rhythmically . . . might be singing,
yanks his guitar strings and stomps
his foot. My ears
don't need this.
The bartender probably waters drinks,
but I send that musician another.
My compliments.
My hope.

– Steve Boint

Rainbow Room

Long haired silhouette
at the end of the bar
drinking vodka
martinis
keeps dangling her hair
at me
smiling
easy prey this one
unhinged
and she gonna be
buck wild.

Strolling over
music too loud
to hear
clicking heels.

But I know
the deliberate sound
all too well
know how
this one
ends.

It's on.

Light specs
fluorescent dust
swirling
light spinning . . .

the eyes always
give it away
words never
need to be
spoken.

Trust me
looks
do kill.

– Lanser Howard

Liar's Bench

Laurie had 3 brothers and these 3 brothers were
the toughest dudes in town. This thought streaked
across my mind as I watched her.

Laurie raised her shot glass, straddling the pool table,
gyrating her body in complete synchronicity with the
music. 2Pac's "How Do You Want It," was banging
from the juke as Laurie screeches these same words
at the top of her lungs.

She throws back the shot and gives two more hip
thrusts for good measure as everyone watches
the spectacle unfold in amazement, especially DJ's
girlfriend who started this whole mess with Laurie.

A tough, pistol of a chick, Laurie has fought the world
her whole life. Not a day went by where she had it
easy. Today was no different.

Gloomy, punch the time clock dive, The Liar's Bench
in Placerville is a hard drinkin', hard livin' hangout
of the Warcry's, a local biker gang. And DJ was the
main man. Everyone bowed down to this dude.
Laurie didn't. In fact, she decided this night to
flirt with him, blowing a kiss to his girlfriend while
hanging off him like a cheap coat.

　"What do you want me to play handsome," Laurie
shrieked over the already loud music.
　"Anything but that N music," DJ shot back.

This infuriated Laurie. She bounced around multiple foster homes, one in which her sole angel savior was a Southern woman. This was the exact reason for her 2Pac song choice, plus she loved the song, and it was now showtime.

So back to the pool table dance. DJ marches over and jerks Laurie by the arm off the table.

"Get your bitch ass down."

Laurie has been in/out of abusive relationships her whole life. Started with her father and years of him touching her up, and most recently the reason for her breakup with her drug dealer boyfriend. She was no stranger to beatings and no way this biker dude was going to lay hands on her now.

"Don't f-ing touch me!"

She kicked DJ between the legs, with boots on and DJ's girlfriend sprang into action like a scalded cat. Billiard balls were scattered, beer mugs were shattered, and hair was pulled back and tattered as a swirling mass of arms, legs and fists spun around like a dirt devil.

DJ grabbed them both not trying to break it up but rather more like transporting and hauling duffel bags out the back door, depositing them both into the back alley.

The rain was pouring down, lit only by a yellow streetlight, as they scrapped and battled it out under the dim light. Laurie quickly ended it and stood up ready for a declaration after wiping away a bad joker-smile red streak of blood across her face.

She looked over to DJ and screamed.

   "Why did you make me play that song, you MOTHER#^*r!!

– Lanser Howard

Burning Bush Bar and Grill

There are lines here:
in the walls narrowing toward that stage,
in the air duct bisecting the ceiling,
in uneven cracks between dry floorboards,
in zigzagging conduit connecting bare bulbs,
in fractures wriggling through painted plaster,
and in the faces of patrons still waiting
for what they can't quite name.

– Steve Boint

Illegal

Through The Underworld's open door, a honey-
smooth voice drifted along grand piano chords as
three girls outside glued, with youth's wistfulness,
their faces to the window.

The piano man sang, and the crowd grew. Several
songs passed. Then, demanding that patrons move
back towards the bar and away from the door, he had
all alcoholic beverages removed from anywhere near
his piano, and invited those three girls in.

Giggling, they sat around the piano, and he sang
to them an old Billy Joel song, *Just the Way You Are*,
and they hung on every word. At the end, he shooed
them out the door and patrons came back around the
piano. Class.

– Steve Boint

Catching Up

You've remained undetected for years,
you and the old crowd.
Now I hear you married rich:
a girl who smiles at sarcasm.
And the others, according to rumor,
have pools, hot tubs;
Jason even has a yacht.
Me?
I'm still drinking in dives
where no chairs match
and tables rest over holes in the floor.
A determined person can nurse one beer for hours
of free air conditioning.
Life drips by and I stay cool.

– Steve Boint

East London Club

Lost and broken.

I hit
rock bottom
but that song resurrected me.

Italian, blonde Russian and
Albanian women
swirling
around me.

Life wasn't so bad.

A year being dead
now
rising to the crescendo
rhythm
of the thousand fluttering
heartbeats
the music
brought me back to life.

But my sweet Albanian,
East London
get down
girl
resurrected me
that night
and
left me
just as fast
under the swirling stars.

I found myself

blurry
upside down
in the Charing Cross Hotel
with nothing
but nickel-flavored
regret
and the red
laser beam light
of a smoke alarm
watching me
piercing the dead silence,
the screaming silence
of night.

But I did find
love
that night
in a hopeless place
just like the song.

I found love
in a steel-willed
place
called belief.

Belief in myself.

– Lanser Howard

Shards

Shards of glass
flashing through shadows
of bodies
frozen in time.

Dance down
empty streets and
faded smiles
burned away in time.

Touch the soul of
a lover
dirty with rhyme
see the eyes of
an angel.

Pray for that
chance
beg for the weight
of flesh
thirst for that
flash
of a chance
to fight
the impossible.

We all want
real
hands
to show us the way
we all grasp
for truth
in our dreams.

We all need
love
to breathe
through
impossibility.

– Lanser Howard

Morning After German Fest

You had more dignity last night
wearing a hat
shaped like
a chicken.

– Steve Boint

The Antler

I remember that moment. Walking into the Antler, while Paddy and Mary waited outside. It was one of the best "marrow of the moment," moments ever.

We all met at a Killarney, Ireland pub. I immediately started talking to Paddy, he was a force of nature with his overwhelming wit and charm. We exchanged rounds as Mary joined the fray. Things were dissolving fast and in overtime, the brilliant idea was hatched.

  "Let's go to the Antler and bring Lans," Paddy exclaimed.
  "Oh, you're an evil one, aren't ya," Mary laughed back.

Great idea. We're all drunk off our asses and I'm in a foreign country. No idea how far away The Antler is and about to trust total strangers with my life. The bar apparently is way out in the Irish countryside.

  "Mate, no way you'll be served. Nobody outside of Killorglin goes here, family only. You may as well walk into a stranger's living room," Paddy blurts out. "It will be great, epic mate!"
  "Yeah, love, I can drive us home," Mary offered up for us to consider the proposition.

And with that, Paddy, Mary and myself walked out of the pub and followed Mary to her car. Blind faith is like riding the wind. You never know where you'll end up but damn it can be fun to roll the dice and find out.

So off we went to Killorglin. Killorglin is best known for the King Puck Summer festival party they throw each year. And in true Irish fashion, the idea of the party is to revel in pure gluttony, have no reservations about having the best time possible.

For the King Puck festival each year, the most adept townsmen go into the nearby mountains and capture a wild goat and bring it back to the town's square where they erect a 20-foot platform and feed the goat all it can eat, all weekend, to see how much it can take in while the party all of Ireland partakes in rages on all weekend. The ultimate celebration of excess. Excess drinking.

The party rocks on and at the end of the weekend, they weigh the mighty goat to see how much weight it gained. Records are kept with ambition to be broken and then the goat is set free back into the mountains.

Time froze as I walked into the Antler. All eyes on me, all movement stopped as I walked up to the bartender, staring daggers at me.

"Give me a shot of Power," I said slapping my hand down onto the bar for extra emphasis. You could have heard a pin drop.

"Mate, you better turn and walk the ..."

And just then, Paddy and Mary swung the front door open.

"Shaun, get me fuckin' mate Lans a drink."

The bar split to pieces laughing as men I didn't know, pushed and pulled my shoulders.

"You got balls mate"
"Aye, fuckin' aye mate"
"You were a dead man"

I did feel like family.

"I'd like you to meet my son," Mary said.

A small, timid boy stepped forward. Too embarrassed to make eye contact.

On the drive over, Mary told me about her divorce and how hard it was on Danny. How losing his father broke him and how he has never been the same. Rebelling against his mother and the world, acting out and getting into fights, basically doing everything to spite his mother trying to do her best to raise him alone.

"Nice to meet you Danny," I shook the boy's hand and motioned for the bartender to bring over a frosty coke for my new friend.
"Your mom tells me you're a pretty good footballer. A little Stevie G (Gerrard)," I continued.
"Well Danny, in school you learn a lot, people will teach you things but there is ONLY one thing you MUST learn and always remember."

I reached down and grabbed his shoulder, giving it a good squeeze, looking him dead in the eye.

"ALWAYS listen to your mom. If you forget everything else you learn in school, NEVER forget that."

His eyes were as big as saucers.

"OK, I will," he nodded back in shock.

And throughout the drinking marathon that night, I'd intermittently stop the conversation I was having.

"Danny, what's the ONLY thing you need to remember?"
"Always, listen to me mum!!"
"Good man . . . if you forget everything else you've learned, what must you always remember?"
"To listen to my mum."

I must have asked him 20 times that night that same question and before I could even finish the sentence, he did it for me.

"Listen to my mum!"

Towards the end of the night, Mary pulled me aside, with a scared look on her face.

"You know, that is the nicest thing anyone has ever done for me." She broke down crying. I didn't know what to do. I just hugged her.

I don't know how I made it home that night. I don't care. All I know is I had one of the best nights of my life – company wise – it's never got any better than that.

Strangers can become family . . . and a young man learned something I hope he never forgot.

– Lanser Howard

The Turtle

The $1,000 punch
happened here.

My man Shaun
was as pure as
they come
funny as hell
life of the party
I called him
the Pirate.

The Pirate could
make you laugh
until your gut
hurt
and The Turtle was his
pirate ship
he was the captain
of every party
any group
always
the life of it.

The Turtle
was HIS spot.

½ dozen rum and cokes
in
Jay and Shaun
got
a bit sideways
f-ing around
out front
throwing hands

slap boxing
to see
who could
take who?

Tempers flared
rum and coke fueled
hands
got heavier and heavier
Jay getting the worst
of it
ends up with
a chipped tooth.

Yells to Shaun
What the F***
you're my friend?!

Grimaces
a jagged
front tooth.

Pirate apologizes
all over
right?

Everyone files back
into the bar
except
Pirate.

Pirate had a very
difficult

life
had understandable
anger issues
lost his mother
lost his brother
both to suicide
slipped on his mother's blood
when he found her
couldn't make it
to that deserted motel
in Sacramento
in time
to get his brother
and best friend
to the ER.

But he always
did his best
tried to help people
never
would hurt anyone
especially a friend.

A crashing wall of glass
everyone
outside
as Pirate stood there
in a daze
lost
staring into the blank space
of his own reflection
he just punched out.

We miss you Pirate
we miss your heart
we miss your unwavering loyalty
but damn it
that was an expensive
and stupid
1,000 dollar punch.

But you were there
the next day
8am
to personally apologize
and hand deliver that $1,000 check
to the mattress store owner.

Stand up guy
a toast to the Pirate
RIP buddy
miss you.

– Lanser Howard

Emily

on the mend and back at work

Behind the counter, she stood:
drugged-up beauty, wavering,
broken nose,
scraped skin,
half-closed eyes.

Run over by some fool.
Sent scrambling for survival.

Life's been doing that to way too many of us lately.

– Steve Boint

Bobby's Beacon

Beacon Light by the Sea
is the only place
I know
where Hill folk . . .
Hills Have Eyes folk
mix
with Hollywood producers
and music elite
and drug cartel
runners
moving weed interstate
south
from the 5
to Highway 1.

And THE man
that runs the show
owns the joint
I call
The Captain
Bobby Beacon.

Bobby married me
had Eric clear out a path
to his beach
with a backhoe
day of
the wedding.

Yes he is an ordained
minister
in addition
to many other talents
he runs the town of Elk

everything that happens
or is planned
in Elk
must run through The Captain.

An honorable man
certified 100%
bad ass
thoroughbred
not a mix of anything
but
heart & soul
and respect.

Saved Rory
he was a ghost
until Bobby stepped in
when trouble came lookin'
for him
that night
at the Beacon
only got his eye
cut out.

The Beacon
sits atop a hill
overlooking the Pacific
easily
the most beautiful
dive bar
in the world
it truly
is "A Room at the Top"
of the world.

Not my words.

Tom Petty
said it better
listen to his song
of the same name
he knows it too
he wrote it
there
after seeing the view.

Bobby's Beacon
is a beacon . . .
it will restore
your faith
and hope
in this world.

To The Captain.

– Lanser Howard

Small Bar In Brasov, Romania

Gone were the days of being able to sell my blue
jeans for a whole month of drinking and eating and
hotel stays. Gone were the days of having waitresses
ask me to, at least, take their dog back to America
so it could have a better life. Gone were the days of
concrete-block construction and abandoned Roman
ruins with nobody walking around them. I sat in this
thrown-together, almost 1990s-style, strip mall in
Transylvania. I didn't miss Ceausescu; I did NOT miss
communist rule, but I did miss the lack of capitalist-
shallow Bauhaus construction. So much had changed.
The formerly impenetrable forest – ripped down, and
the castles – now tourist traps. So much had been
lost; so much had been gained. At least in this bar
they still had those great Romanian hard rolls. I don't
know how they make them: the crust is so hard on
the outside; the inside is so soft, delicious. And their
drinks were about the same as everywhere else –
alcohol. So I was content.

– Steve Boint

The Alpine

I was looking for an old friend in a beat-up old bar.
He wasn't there that day, but I hoped to find out if he
still frequented the place. I asked the bartender. She
had never seen him, or at least she didn't admit to
having seen him.

Then the tall guy with no hair, sitting right beside
where I was standing, slurred, "A little short guy
with a lot of hair above and below his eyes?"

Yeah, that's him.

"Haven't seen him."

And so it went.

– Steve Boint

Chemist In a Bar

Between sips of "Red",
the only wine this place offers,
she wonders why slow poison
has such profound emergent effects
on highly-evolved intelligence.

Alcohol. Tobacco. Psychedelics.
How many musicians, writers, artists
only produce good stuff when high?
Has anyone compared the quality of
sober vs stoned paintings by chimps?

– Steve Boint

A Single Drunk Voice Behind Me at Open Mic Night

so is it chaotic
sitting toward the front
why'd you want to sit up there
when there was a seat here
it's Cajun man
ironically frugal
magic
it's a learning disorder
it's Cajun
what the hell's wrong with you
it's magic

– Steve Boint

The Dungeon

If you want
to know
what it feels like
to go
down a rabbit hole
walk into The Dungeon
in New Orleans.

Step into
the abyss
and feel
the landslide
of metal
hammer you
in a pouring down
rain
of metal music.

There are no other
options.

Nothing else exists
on the juke.

So buckle up
for the fast and
furious ride
of speed metal
and shots
served up
like machine gun splatter.

Maybe
that is why
they call it
The Dungeon
as you
will be tortured
beyond
your wildest dreams
if you can't appreciate
the raw
cold rifts of metal
and machine gun
splatter
of heavy drums.

Carnage of metal
in its highest
form
destruction of sanity
taken
to an art form.

– Lanser Howard

Premonition

Below bare-wire ball and tube,
with a candle's flicker, a dim bulb illumines:
the bartender wiping a cup with . . .
    his shirt?
a disinterested red-head scuffing lines in the dirty
    floor tile,
an old, whiskered man watching from beside,
    maybe, his wife.
You are not here,
yet.

– Steve Boint

Saturday night,

another,
like all the others.
Same bar as last week.
One more too-talented band
playing for too little.
Few listen.
It's OK;
tonight she is with me
and I'm happy.

– Steve Boint

The Black Rose

U2's *Bad* song broke
immediately
memories
rushing back
the landslide of loss
buried me
in that military
drumming of Mullen.

The fluorescent
eerie red
glow of the Red Hook
sign
bled and blurred
lines
of reality
as I sank
deeper
into that cellar
chill
of lost love.

I knew
IT
now was gloriously
OVER
just in time
for that final drum break
of *Bad* . . .

20 years
up in flames.

– Lanser Howard

The Dirty Lowdown Dogs

This place? Not bad, really,
but ragtime doesn't require
opposable thumbs
or large frontal lobes.

Overwhelming enthusiasm?
They've got it!
Strong need to run?
O yeah!

Not at all like modern jazz bars
spotted with intellectuals
nodding
at some cat on a keyboard.

– Steve Boint

Hemingway Bar

The confetti rained down and the kazoos rang out as
I sat, looking at the bathroom door waiting, waiting
for her to come out. Everything was in slow motion
as I sat frozen in a trance, waiting for that door to
open so I could ring in the New Year with my new
acquaintance.

But the door never opened. She walked in and never
came out. A ghost. A brilliant "I gotta go to the
bathroom" disappearing act.

   "Where did Lilly go," her friend yelled over the
music, sandwiched between her newfound boyfriend.

We were at a Key Largo Hemingway dive. One of his
favorite haunts after wrestling marlins all day. A
place fisherman roll in to tell tales of that big one
that got away over shots and cold beer.

Well another big one did get away.

She was beautiful, looked like Esmeralda with a
girl next door flair. Lilly was sincere, talked about
moving to the Keys with her daughter to start
over after a long, abusive relationship. We drank
margaritas for hours, really hit it off which made her
disappearing act that much more puzzling.

Only one conversation point that didn't hit the mark.
She had a daughter. I didn't have kids.

The universe has a funny way of weeding out mismatches. This was a colossal one, only problem was I was the only one that didn't see it.

Hindsight is always 20/20.

So the clock struck 12 and I struck out. I still sat there frozen, staring at that bathroom door nobody was walking back through. The New Year's song started to play.

In between that moment when the confetti was falling like snow and the music paused for 'old acquaintances,' I realized one thing. I'm alone . . . all alone at a time you should never be alone. After the clock strikes 12 on New Year's.

The next thing I remember, I was driving down a one-way dirt road, way out on the island. Nothing but the sound of the waves licking up against those jagged mangrove roots. I can still hear it.

I was lost in the mangroves, and I lost my mind.

– Lanser Howard

Alone

My soul screeches in high corners,
skitters across long walls,
brushes two patrons gulping liquor,
pauses briefly near that blonde waitress,
then writhes beneath tables.
I stare at my sandwich, body still.
It's OK;
no one will notice.

– Steve Boint

Tuesday Night

One of the gray ones
now, an uninteresting lump
on a too-hard stool,
he glances past a bartender
into the looking
glass behind clean mugs and bottles.
There he is again . . .
that wrinkled man watching him drink.
As if synchronized,
they toast past, present, and future.

– Steve Boint

Far Too Late

A little bar, one-third of a block south and across
the street, that's where I became aware of how cold
a city can be. As our sun dropped behind too-tall
apartments in the west, in front of that bar a small
struggle left one local teenager shot and dying on the
sidewalk almost blocking the door. The neighbors
kept stepping over him to go inside for drinks. And
people were coming out of the bar, drinks in hand,
pizza slices in hand, stepping over the kid and then
standing there and drinking and eating and talking
and watching him die. He was entertainment. By the
time the ambulance and the police arrived, as per
usual, it was too late.

– Steve Boint

Not a Sleepy Bar

And they all chatter.
The singers sing,
bang their guitars.

At the counter,
the big guy bangs his beer bottle,
roars something to the brunette two chairs away.

That crash when the bartender tossed the empty
made me jump.

In the corner,
a small guy in fedora stares
at his drink.

The lady at table next
just grabbed her breasts,
exclaimed, "Oh!"

Wonder what the small guy said.

– Steve Boint

McNally's

Hands down the best
Irish pub
in the East Bay
McNally's
in Oakland.

So many days
the early days
I spent here
many of my secrets
are buried here
Tony being the only
witness.

So many good times . . .
far too many
Harps and
Jameson shots and
Slain
when Tony got the order right
that week.

I found the fuel for my voice
as a writer
here
the people, the faces
everything
McNally's had it all

best being
only a short walk
home
usually
loaded
I'd make it
to write it all out.

So much history here . . .
and one of the best barmen
Tony
the wittiest and wiliest
bartender alive
retired now
thank God
as he tried to charm
every woman I brought in
but always
doled out free drinks
to her
not me
and kept the secrets
of your bad nights
but
always
let you hear about it
next time you were in for a pint.

McNally's
a landmark
THE neighborhood bar
in Rockridge
still the only pub
to watch all the World Cup
or Euro games
no matter the time
McNally's is always open
you just better
root for Ireland
or
suffer the consequences.

– Lanser Howard

Drove Here Alone

A purple hoodie lurches in,
scans the room looking for something,
settles for a bar stool.

Conversation slithers around corner booths.

Opposite the bar,
a comb-over plays music from the depths of space
on a saw. Strangely amazing.

As my designated driver,
I settle for coffee.

– Steve Boint

George & Walts

An old bowling alley
George & Walts
is the spot.

Gangsters, gamblers
businessmen
drunks
all mingle together.

Everyone is
ONE.

Nobody is
better
than the next
man.

Crowd
turns over
late night.

Whole new world
opens up.

Names I can't
name
regularly
roll through here.

Some famous
did their dirt
here.

The best of
times
for me
and the worst of
times
I've spent here.

My writing career
started here
I ended many
far too many
nights
here
sometimes with company
most times
alone
back when
I was alone
it was the only place
I had
when I had
nothing.

George & Walts
is in my blood
and soul
forever
open for business.

– Lanser Howard

King's Cross

It was a narrow escape. A band of Pikeys had us at
the King's Cross, a wild reckless bar in the heart of
Amsterdam.

But we must go back to the beginning and how
it all went wrong. The misfortune all started
upon meeting Thorston, a big German Viking,
and probably the funniest dude I ever met. When
someone is as funny as Thorston, it's a superpower.
He can influence you to do things you normally
wouldn't do in a million years.

"It's just a spliff, harmless," Thorston said.
"Well, I promised Michelle I wouldn't partake in
the magical herb. It's different level here, no joke,
everyone knows that."
"Dude, it's got tobacco, it's half and half. You'll be
fine."

Then I took the first step into complete, utter
oblivion and the last step of what I remembered
for the rest of the night. I stepped out of the bar
with Thorston, took a hit of the magical blunt and
immediately an 18-wheeler roared up, inside me.

The rest of the story and what happened was told
to me by my Dutch friends and our fearless German
leader.

A gnome-like man, the size of a Keebler elf, had pints
waiting for us as Thorston and I plunked ourselves
back down at the table.

"Whatever you do Lans, do NOT look at that painting," Keebler man exclaimed.

Everyone laughed as the conversation got fragmented into separate tales of the unknown and bad luck for those stupid enough to look at what I can only describe as an orgy of a blonde woman and six wild tigers engulfing her. I know this because yes, I looked at the painting.

"C'mon man, that cheap painting. You guys are full of shit."

A heavy silence fell over the party.

"Let's go to King's!!" Thorston roared, pounding his beer down.

Pints were drained as everyone got up and followed our fearless leader to the infamous King's Cross.

Only four of us made it. But that is the definition of Amsterdam nights. A group of many sets out for a particular destination but ultimately only half make it as the magic allure of the city pulls you in separate directions.

All eyes on us as we entered into the dark, King's Cross which seemed to have a family of people in it. People that all knew one another, people that ultimately would all play their parts in an elaborate play. A play on us.

Pikeys are no joke. Bad ass bandits that have been

conning and robbing people for centuries. You don't fuck with them. More brutal and worse than the mob.

Tomas immediately made friends with Michelle. Well built, and tatted up, Tomas was funny and a nice guy . . . in the beginning . . . and then he full on, started full court pressing Michelle. His mother, Liv, was a different story. Drunk off her ass, she kept grabbing at Michelle's breasts and grind dancing sloppily behind her.

The bartender made eye contact with Tomas, as he nodded back and 3 more shots of whiskey arrived.

   "Mate, I was in the traveling circus. I was the clown, did it for years . . . now we're just a traveling band," Tomas proclaimed.
   "Are all these crew guys then," Thorston motioned towards several guys leaning against the back wall of the bar.

And then, I noticed it through my inebriated haze, a big dude against the wall nodded to a guy in back, stationed near the back door. How I had the clarity to pick this up in my wrecked state, I don't know. My spider senses usually don't fail me when I sense something is about to go down. All my friends were drunk and having a really good time, no way I'm getting us out of here anytime soon. And then, the first few notes broke, and utter madness ensued.

"Just a small-town girl. Livin' in a lonely world. He took the midnight train going anywhere. . ."

The whole bar chimed in, everyone singing at the top of their lungs as the party was in full swing. Liv grabbed Michelle by the hand, pulling her to the top of the bar, Tomas flanked her as both were grinding her from both sides. A sandwich I need to figure out how to break up, fast.

Thorston found himself a cute pikey girl, now spinning her around and all I can think of is how quick we can get the hell out of here.

Tomas is a street dude. He knows the look of concern if you show it. He noticed I noticed the dude nodding.

"Tomas, my man, I'm buying the next round. What do ya want?"

He eyeballed me but I convinced him.

"Mate, get me another Jager shot . . . I gotta take a piss."

He strolled off to the bathroom. It was then I had to make my move. I pulled Michelle down off the bar, pushed Thorston toward the door and whispered to him.

"It's gonna get ugly if we don't leave now. Just trust me."

I pushed the big man towards the door and took Michelle by the hand in tow. Luckily, Thorston being a massive Viking, gave us an advantage vs the lone Moroccan mafioso guy, standing between us and freedom.

"Where you guys going, party just started," the Moroccan deadpanned as he stepped into our path to the door.

"We're out homie" . . . but the brilliance was in the stone-cold delivery of that line. And all so subtle step forward, not crowding, but getting ever so slightly up into the grill of the Moroccan just enough to back him off.

I swung the door open, and I swear I felt like a bird that just flew the coop.

We found out later how lucky we were to get out of that jackpot.

Apparently, a band of Swedish Pikeys were back in town, trapping and robbing unsuspecting tourists at the King's Cross. They paid off the owner to let them run their game. Invite people in, get them drunk, then lock the front and back doors as the Pikey party turns into an absolute horror show.

Easy pickings for the Pikeys to beat up and rob with all the alcohol consumed. King's owner benefits too from both the money on shots/drinks and the Pikeys overall take.

No wonder why the furniture was cleared out while we were drinking and singing "Don't Stop Believing."

We got lucky. Believe that.

– Lanser Howard

Small Town Bar

And it's a long way back from a feeble sun,
hungry wind, ice-encrusted . . .
everything.
Hands bigger than his beer glass,
calloused, like his eyes.
Neither warms the other, she decides,
polishing the far end of her bar.
It's been a long time since warmth
accompanied any of her customers.

With the last one ejected,
north wind howls
and the cooling building pops, chuckles –
the most meaningful conversation of the night.

– Steve Boint

The Other Side Bar
for C.L.

Like being in a railroad car,
same proportions, same decor –
that old beat-up bar
across from the abandoned post office.

Why he went there, he didn't know
but, usually, someone knew him
and those nights were at least not lonely.

Posters on the wall really just beer ads.
A back door that led to a smoking section,
which he didn't need, himself,

but would sometimes follow someone through,
just keeping up the conversation.
It was a friendly place.

Five years after the pandemic,
he went back and woke up in a jail cell.
The police said they held him just for observation;

someone must have slipped him a mickey
and beat him unconscious in the alley behind that bar.
They didn't even steal his wallet.
He's never been back.

– Steve Boint

The Golden West

Fort Bragg's finest
since the 1800's
THE Golden West.

Bar better named
Wild West.

A former brothel
saloon
with a special feature
a cozy jail cell
in back
for those who step outta line.

First thing I noticed
was a hole
punched
in the men's room
door
just another Saturday night
last night.

Gravel lot out back
back
in the Fight Club
days
popped off
now
just an overflow spot
for Friday night
grievances.

Good dive
bar
drinks are
bottle up
strong.

– Lanser Howard

Crowded Bar On Northland Ave.

Plastic baggies pass over and under
tables loaded with greasy chicken and paper cups.
No exit, only a gauntlet –
bulletproof plexi along the north wall
makes a hallway with a door:
buzz to get in, buzz to get out.
Surreptitiously, I slip
my credit card and license into my shoe.

– Steve Boint

Full Circle: Another Holiday Season

Crystal jalapeños splash hot color on black walls,
artwork of peace and struggle.
Authors framed by time refuse to grin
from above the bar. Talk flows of tats and shops,
nothing in particular, Jesus, the Maccabees,
hope and how light glows briefly these days.
Colored reflections in eyes hint at family stories.
People of the street don't feel distant and
outside
falling snow whispers poems.

– Steve Boint

The Central

Still the best bar
downtown
to get a cold Ranier
and shot.

Since the 1800's
The Central Saloon
in Pioneer Square
has been the nerve center
for music
and good times.

Saw the Melvins
Mother Love Bone
and listened to Slaves and Bulldozers
break here
in the hollow
fluorescent moonlight.

Oceans rose up
heavens opened up
as the grunge tide
rolled in
Jesus
first
sang his glorious song
here
and changed the world.

Soundgarden
ignited
a swirling mass
of long hair
and good times
that
has never left
still rolls on today.

You want heaven
with a touch
of hell.

Visit The Central.

– Lanser Howard

Art and Music

Triangle Bar,
again . . .
between sets,
asked the lead if I could photograph
the band
to use for a painting.
He reached out,
shook my hand,
"No."

– Steve Boint

Blues

Rap music bites
my ears.

Whiskey bites
my tongue.

Steel chair bites
my ass.

Should have bought
a cookie.

– Steve Boint

September Saturday Night

Beside me, she sketches.
The band fumbles.
Bottles and laughter pile up
    on that table across from ours.
Bouncer dozes at his door seat,
    nose dropping closer and closer
    to the change drawer.
A grey man at the bar kisses the side of his bottle;
    drains it.
An urban square dance
    of paths crossing between
    tables, counter, restrooms
    remains collision-free.
I relax, finally.
Beside me, she sketches.

– Steve Boint

White Pines Bar

Mountains
lose me
wicked darkness
screams through
open windows.

Thoughts leave behind
fear.

Alpine air burns
the brain
as the sun
dreams again.

I am home
at last
free
and at peace
once again.

– Lanser Howard

Patterson's

"What we drinkin'."

Michelle nodded toward a frosty, vodka martini served up to a woman the size of an ox.

"OK, it's gonna be one of those civilized nights," I proclaimed.

And right then, the bar stool next to me slid out and down sat skater man wearing a slick, flat billed, bejeweled Dodgers hat. I glanced down to my side as a massive, slobbering beast plunked down beside me.

"Looks like he likes the ladies," I said.
"Oh yeah, and nobody f**ks with me when I bring him here," skater man replied.

Michelle and I exchanged smiles.

"Well, I have a chihuahua," Michelle blurts out.

Oh man, here we go.

"Chihuahuas are stupid dogs," skater man huffs as he takes a man-sized pull of his beer, clanking it down onto the bar to impress us with his authority.
"Pits are smarter and big dogs in general make much better companions than little dogs."

I knew Michelle wouldn't let this one sit.

"Well, I used to have 2 chihuahuas and 1 of them,

actually the smaller of the two, went after a pit bull and scared it off after it tried to attack my other dog."

"No way. No way a chihuahua would scare a pit, let alone try to fight it. Little dogs are scared of big dogs."

The conversation just got ratcheted up a notch. We sat in silence pondering that question before our flat-billed idiot huffed and reached down, slapping the barrel chest of his prized brute.

"Big dogs are better," he said staring at Michelle.
"BIG . . . but you're such a LIT-TLE guy," she replied, wincing as if in pain.

And with that, the little man had enough. He jumped up, snapped the leash of his big, bad dog, slammed down his beer and headed for the door.

"You're just a BIG meanie!!"

Everyone laughed as the door swung open and ant man left. And just like that, Patterson's little, big, Pit man was gone.

– Lanser Howard

A Sort of Rapture

Across the street, barely
readable in midday's glare:
JESUS SAVES SINNERS
but
the church is gone and that sign rises
    at the corner of asphalt and grit
    where cars now rest.
From the false dusk of The Rusty Bar's wall,
I watch a dog brave dust devils to mark the promise.

– Steve Boint

The Darkening Clock

It feels late
and she sits
under a false strobe –
a recessed LED bulb
failing spastically –
and she drinks
inside this crumbling bar
in this crumbled industrial district
in this crumbling city.
At this time of night,
what else would she do,
where else would she be?

– Steve Boint

LBC Ghetto Dive

Nothing but a constant
humming of cars
sometimes I wonder
if
there is ever any silence
in these brutal streets.

All the screaming
lies
tense
muffled tonight
like a poised tiger
waiting
unleashing
bottled fury
cleansing torment
releasing anger.

For when night
falls
bright lights
smiles fade
and out come the demons
crawling
wreaking havoc
fear
spreading like a disease
over its victim

leaving them
cold
anxious
tense
as they grip
the covers
ever so tightly
and stir restlessly
in bed
as another siren
pierces the silence
of the night.

– Lanser Howard

Gang Territory Mandolin Nights

Every couple months, we'd place the wheels and battery of our car at risk; head south on Broad Street about halfway to the old stadium, and then west into gang territory. Late evening, we'd pull up and park on the street outside a little row house on the north end of a block. The front door had been nailed shut, but the side door was open-ish – a one-person-wide hallway had been built along the length of the east side of the building so that on the south end of the house you could walk into the passageway and then get to the side door of the house. People, including gangs, could only come in one person at a time. Although the roof of the building was ringed by razor wire, inside, the ground floor of this two-story home had been converted into a restaurant. The south room was kitchen; middle was the dining area; the front, behind that nailed-in door, was the bar. And we'd sit in that bar and listen to old man Strolli play his mandolin, and we'd talk to each other and listen some more and talk to each other. An amazing sight, this skinny old guy with Coke-bottle eyeglasses, a big cigar sticking out of his mouth, humming softly through little clouds, playing his mandolin and ignoring everybody else. Around us, people talked, jostled their way back to the bar, and took a chair when one became available. Wish we could go back.

– Steve Boint

106

Never Learned the Name of That Place

In the back of an old hotel, a little restaurant/
bar in Giurgiu, beneath hanging chandeliers from
the Ceausescu era (they'd cost a year's salary now,
back then they were standard), I drank beside an
old man who, between drinks, chewed on food I
had never seen before. This was Romania, so it was
probably a combo of pork and cabbage and vinegar.
He'd ask me about America; I'd ask him about his
life, and we'd toast each other. In the mid 1970s, his
mother cleaned the street they lived on in Bucharest
– everybody had a job, no matter how minimal,
back then. It was a very busy street and, in early
mornings, she would wait for the light to turn red,
run out with a bucket of water and a broom. When
the light turned green and cars surged forward, she
had to dive to get out of the way and back on the
sidewalk. Sometimes she'd lose her bucket in the
traffic . . . or her broom. But he said it's better now.
He had a little boat and ran tours on the Danube.
Mostly it was a floating bar, people were happy.
But one time he had a group of pensioners from the
town of Oroiu, and they asked him to shut off the
motor and just drift with the flow of the Danube. As
we raised a glass to progress and tourists, he added,
"That's the thing about Romania nowadays, you just
wouldn't think of doing that."

– Steve Boint

Midnight At the Triangle Bar

Neon bicycle
with its FAT TIRE mounted on
the bowed plaster wall.

Plastered patrons perch
on stools or cling knuckles
white to wood tables.

This crowd won't walk out,
maybe crawl, but the door keeps
moving; the floor too.

The band plays on.

– Steve Boint

Big Night At the Basement Bar

Alcohol.
Wild music.
Whirring fans.
Madly flickering candles on each table.
What could go wrong?

– Steve Boint

Dante's

Dante's Inferno
is not in hell
it resides in Portland
downtown
stroll from civilization
to pure out-of-bounds
bedlam.

On its worst night
pure hell
a freak show
of people
fire eaters
a sad clown
with knives in his back
playing a rainbow-colored accordion
smiling.

At a moment's notice
a steel plate
the size of a banquet table
ignites
into a wall of fire
floor to ceiling.

You are in hell.

On its best night
like a woman
it will please
you
in ways unexplained
but felt
deep to your core
pleasures
do exist
in this material world
but only
within the nine planes
of Dante's Inferno.

The one
in Portland.

– Lanser Howard

El Toro Negro
Prague

The eyes dry heave too
when you have lost
so much
there is no more
to give . . .
you can't even
shed a tear.

Death back home
all alone
in the dark zone
in Prague.

The rock
basement
bottom
I promise you
you don't know the chill
until you face
the eyes of the dead
swirling
all around you.

You know
then
then
it crystallizes.

Your dreams.
Your fears.

Wait and
watch the rain
drip
drop
listen to the
tick
tock
and wait for
the glock
to click
clock
into something better.

– Lanser Howard

First Day of Rehab

"It'll be my last drink."

We both looked at each other in disbelief. Is this really f-ing happening? We were on our way to drop JL off and check him into rehab.

"I'm going away guys."

JL then broke down, collapsing to the ground like a heap of wet cement.

"I can't do this. I've never f-ing been alone in my life. F*** man, last 4 years I've been on a boat in the middle of the Pacific. The Navy did this to me."
"JL, c'mon man, remember in high school . . . that Antioch party you did the Humpty Dance . . . slick shuffle except for side-stepping into the pool."

We all busted up, laughing but then stopped abruptly. The gravity of the situation took hold of us all. I was the first to hug JL.

"You can do this J. And damn, imagine all the weight you'll lose."

We all got fidgety and sat there wondering the obvious. JL was not a disciplined man, he gets caught up in the moment, same flow of the moment that put him in a swimming pool last time he heard the Humpty Dance.

I have never felt the aching silence of a moment more significantly than that parting of ways. How the light fractured those lonely oak branches reaching up to a broken sky. Birds sang as we sat there for what seemed like an eternity.

"Guys . . . thanks for doing this. If I can do it, I'll do it for you."

Silence obliterated. Hope lit back up the sun.

"OK then, let's go get that last drink against our better judgment. This was always your favorite dive bar," Joe said as we resigned ourselves to the inevitable.

I put my arm around JL as we walked off into a place JL wouldn't be seeing for a very long time.

STP's *Creep* started playing on the juke the minute we stepped into the bar. First line of that song rang out "Forward yesterday, makes me want to stay. . ."

I'm still haunted by those lyrics to this day.

– Lanser Howard

Bar Los Juanes
Seville

It takes a day
maybe two
to decompress from the coming
and going.

So much to see
in this beautiful city.

You don't wanna
stop
blink
and miss it.

No sights or sounds
you remotely know
the first day is always about
finding your heart
where you left it
in the distant memories
of yesterday.

Cobblestone replaces pavement
in Sevilla
no horns
only the easy notes of a distant
guitar whispering
two *calles* down.

My exhale . . .

Red vino
albondigas y tapas.

I'm finally home
away
from home.

– Lanser Howard

To Answer That Question:

like sitting down
in a sparse bar,
two old men
beside the floor lamp
strum electric ukelins
and hum tattered memories.
Behind them hangs my portrait
though I don't recognize it
and didn't pose for it.
That's how this birthday felt.

– Steve Boint

Between Bitter and Sullen

Silence shadows these patrons.
Eyes accidentally lock,
dart elsewhere.
Faces bend toward lottery hopes
or dying phones.
Not that long ago the corner booth buzzed:
clipped calls, stream of wraiths.
Don't ask: empty for months.
No one removes their coat
and laughter no longer walks through.

– Steve Boint

The Turf

"Billy is that you?"

We were greeted with that question from the owner upon walking into The Turf. A fine establishment in Sundance, Wyoming where my father tended bar as a young man. 50 years later, he wanted to buy me a drink from a bar that once was in our family. We wouldn't be buying anything today.

"Yes, it's me Karen. You were the toughest boss I ever had."

Hugs were exchanged.

"You don't look a day past 50 . . . a lot better than me," Karen declared.
"Still a whiskey drinker?" She picked up a bottle of Jim Beam, poised and ready.
"And the young man looks thirsty too."
"Thanks Karen, so nice to see you again."

She poured us both Atlantic Ocean sized shots.

"So this was our bar? Never knew we had a bar in the family. I woulda came out to Sundance a lot sooner."

Karen laughed and rolled her eyes at my Dad.

"Billy had all the girls chasing him. I swear on the nights he worked; we doubled our sales. Melted 'em with that dimpled smile and being a cowboy."
"Stop it Karen . . . my son doesn't need to hear any of those stories."

We all toasted the Jim Beam.

"Well now, how about the pig roast when Billy had one too many."

"OK, I gotta hear this one," I shot back.

"Yep, Billy had the BBQ going out back, under that Cedar tree. He got to talking and drinking too much instead of tending the grill."

Dad started laughing hysterically.

"I forgot about that one," he said.

Karen poured another two shots.

"So what happened," I begged.

"Well, what happened was the whole tree went up in flames, caught hold of the bar and The Turf damn near burned to the ground."

We all laughed.

"Did it burn down?" I asked.

"No, the Fire department made it here in time and saved things." Karen said.

"And I had to spend the next 3 years working for free to pay off the damages," Dad replied. "I tried to sell that collection there to help pay off the debt."

He motioned up to the collection of Lionstone Whiskey bottles carefully setup over the bar.

"At the time, it was the only Lionstone full collection anywhere in the US but your grandfather wouldn't let me, had to teach me a lesson."

And to this day, The Turf still hosts wild Friday and Saturday nights, still the best watering hole in Sundance. Pay it a visit, if you ever get up there.

The Lionstone Whiskey collection still stands guard over the bar. It survived the fire but unfortunately the arson who started the fire didn't.

We had a toast that day to both his old turf and The Turf.

Good times.

– Lanser Howard

Bleeding Time

Blood spills all
over
time.

Take a walk with
me
and I'll tell
you
what I see.

I see the rich
rot in the blaze
of time.

I see the eyes
of the living dead
swirling
around me.

If you come with
me
I'll show you.

See the weak
over there
trying to murder
pain.

Look in here
and you'll see
the desperate
clinging
to the bones of
prosperity.

Truth swirls
all around us
tonight.

Walk with me over here
and I'll show you
the forgotten ones
if you have the
stomach
to bear it.

See those stone walls
of this abandoned
church. . .
they tell the story
of the homeless,
of the fits of
madness
and pain
you could never
imagine
to just make it
through
another night.

They haunt
this city
these homeless camps
of loneliness
of lost lives
littered everywhere.

Time spits
in our faces
we can never
wipe away
the pain.

So remember
these things
when
you drive through
my city.

Don't judge the
outside
unless you walk
through
the inside
of truth.

– Lanser Howard

The Roundup

Fluorescent beer lights
bleed
good times
every night
The Roundup in Lafayette
rounds up
a barn
full of all types.

Every Friday and Saturday night
the crowd
turns over
drink after work
9 to 5ers
to locals
to bikers . . .
everyone imaginable
hangs
here
and is rounded up
for a good time.

My girl Roxanne
runs the show
an angel in disguise
she takes care of everyone
took care of me
many nights
when I had nothing
but her beautiful
heart and smile
and energy
to help me
through the night.

Ahhh the Roundup . . .
too many
good times to remember
so many
people
I'll never forget.

A good dive
becomes part of
your soul
unexplainable
a home
always
to come back to
but never
leave
at the same time.

This is The Roundup.

– Lanser Howard

Art In the Basement Bar
for SE

He waited tables there and,
finally,
got to hang three of his own
paintings
above corner booths.

He watched patrons react and
glance
his way . . . those who knew his name.
Saw
a drunk guy pull out a marker,

so he pulled out his phone and
caught
Betty Page (space-suited on the moon)
growing
a thick, curled mustache.

Management called police and
court
was avoided through a sobering
purchase.
Most the artist ever made on a single piece.

– Steve Boint

Half Moon Over One More Boarded-Up Bar

Drowning the Harleys, a rebuilt, woody
Grand Wagoneer guns past **JILLS BEERS & BURGERS**.
Eatery at my back: "**1/2 OFF**" three feet high
on the window – same price all year.
Nothing's as advertised.
Even Luna's really a quarter.

– Steve Boint

Coles

Memories are like
oceans
you think of the times
and they rise
and fall
bubble up
faces
places
you breathe them in.

They just come to you
involuntarily
enter your bloodstream.

Warm and good
or cold and bad
no jacket required.

And time to brave it
like it
or not
and this is that
dive
no runnin' for cover
brother
you're in the great
wide open
the floodgates
are open
the levy has
broken
long ago here.

No wonder
Bukowski
loved this place.

The urinal
has his name
to prove it.

– Lanser Howard

Problem With the Door

The door hasn't opened,
not since I slunk in
suddenly wrapped in warm humid
as winter was shoved back by that red door
maybe three hours past.
Three wet hours
and the poster wall grows intriguing:
Profane Saints, Petrified Man, and Champagne Beauty . . .
something about a coffee and donut ride . . .
can't read the remaining from here anymore.
Barkeep is drunk, jovial,
chuckling to the clock by the fridge.
A rumpled blonde clutches Samuel Adams,
rocks, stares at her Android.
Some lanky guy in the dim booth reads.
And
where
were
you?
The door never opened.

– Steve Boint

Mesmerized

Sat
here
watching the tabletop reflection shimmy
    an incorporeal veil dance
    in time with the overhead fan.
My cellphone
buzzed,
    chattered another dance on the tabletop.
Wrong number.

– Steve Boint

Last Call

The last ticks of the clock
empty the heart. . .

This is the way it goes
when destiny ceases to flow
and the mind lays trapped and exposed
down a one-way road.

The last ticks of the clock
separate the black sheep from the flock
and soon time stands still
and the lonely guts start to spill.

Because my friend
the enemy is always the clock
and soon even
the optimistic heart slows to a stop.

For on the last ticks of the clock
the bar spills out onto the block
and only your memories
cease to stop.

– Lanser Howard

About the Authors

Lanser Howard began his career as a journalist and then transitioned into film where he wrote and produced an award-winning documentary film *Fight Life* among other screenplays. His sole focus now is on poetry and prose with his first full-length book of poetry *The Screaming Silence* released in 2020.

An Oakland, California, native now living in the Sacramento area, Howard travels the country selling food products by day, writer at night. He has a passion for the outdoors and escapes to the mountains or ocean every chance he gets with his wife Michelle and fearless dog Donovan, aka Booger.

Howard's visceral, minimalistic style paints hard-hitting portraits of the dark and the wounded and seeks to illuminate the struggles of everyday people fighting insurmountable odds. His writing has been featured on *Good Day Sacramento* TV, *Style Magazine* and other publications and various podcasts.

Instagram: @lanserhoward

Steve Boint, owner of Scurfpea Publishing, taught high school chemistry, physics, astronomy as well as adjunct undergraduate astronomy, general chemistry, and vocational organic and biochemistry. He is currently largely retired, but does teach adjunct undergraduate English.

Boint's poetry has been published in several anthologies including *South Dakota In Poems* (edited by Christine Stewart-Nunez, then Poet Laureate of South Dakota). His books of poetry include *Backyard Jubilee* with South Dakota Poet of Merit Charles Luden, *Stranded wherever I am: poems of motels and roads*, and *winddance*.

When not renovating his 150-year-old house, he can be found beside his charcoal-gray Maine coon cat sneaking through his backyard, surprising rabbits, squirrels, opossums, and birds.